Hegel & Hobbes Have an Adventure

iUniverse books may be ordered through booksellers or by contacting:

iUniverse
1663 Liberty Drive
Bloomington, IN 47403
www.iuniverse.com
1-800-Authors (1-800-288-4677)

Because of the dynamic nature of the Internet, any web addresses or links contained in this book may have changed since publication and may no longer be valid. The views expressed in this work are solely those of the author and do not necessarily reflect the views of the publisher, and the publisher hereby disclaims any responsibility for them.

ISBN: 978-1-5320-9970-0 (sc)
ISBN: 978-1-5320-9971-7 (e)
ISBN: 978-1-5320-9972-4 (sc)

Library of Congress Control Number: 2020907896

Print information available on the last page.

iUniverse rev. date: 05/05/2020

Book design by Matt Finlay.

Illustrated by Sarah Drake.

Hegel & Hobbes

HAVE AN ADVENTURE

H egel the hedgehog rose one morning and greeted the sun. His smile was bright as he stepped through his front door and into the garden. Today would be a wonderful day, a fun day. And if he was lucky, he would see his friend Hobbes the hamster and maybe even get a chance to cheer him up.

For Hobbes was not a very happy hamster. Hegel and Hobbes had known each other for a long time, and it seemed Hegel was always trying to cheer up Hobbes. Once in a while he would succeed and bring a smile to Hobbes' face, perhaps with a riddle or clever rhyme. But mostly Hobbes just walked about pouting.

Just as Hegel the hedgehog was thinking these things about his friend, there came a scratching sound at the garden gate. Only one creature in the garden made such a noise. He opened the gate, and, sure enough, there stood Hobbes, wearing a sad face and looking like nothing on earth could make him smile.

"Hello, Hobbes," said Hegel. "Isn't it a wonderful day?!"

"No, not at all. It's a very grim day," replied Hobbes. "I could hardly bring myself to get out of bed."

"Why, Hobbes," declared Hegel. "You cannot really believe such a thing."

"Of course I can," Hobbes said. "Why should today be different from any other day?"

"But Hobbes, just look at the sky. It's blue as can be."

Hegel took Hobbes by the arm, taking care not to poke his friend with his stiff hairs. For everyone knows that hamsters are soft and fluffy, but hedgehogs are covered with stiff and pointy hairs. Sticking his friend with sharp hairs was not going to make Hobbes feel better.

As the two friends walked up the garden path toward Hegel's house, a tiny voice came from the ground below.

"Take care, you brutes," the voice said, so low they could barely hear it.

"You almost stepped on my wagon of seeds."

"Who said that?" asked Hegel.

"Who indeed?" said Hobbes.

"Me indeed," came the tiny voice from down by their feet.

Hobbes and Hegel knelt and put their faces almost to the ground.

"Good heavens," Hegel exclaimed. "It's an ant!"

"Not just any ant," the tiny creature replied. "I am Immanuel, and you very nearly upset my load of seeds, you great beast."

"How odd," Hobbes said, peering closer. "An ant that speaks."

"*I'm* odd?" said Immanuel with great disgust. "Whoever heard of a talking hamster?"

"There, you see," said Hegel looking up at Hobbes with a smile. "The day has only just begun and already we've met a new friend."

"Friend?" asked Hobbes, gazing at the sky with a sigh. "What on earth would I want a friend for?"

"Oh, Hobbes, whyever not?" asked Hegel. "A friend is the very best thing anyone could ask for."

"Speaking of friends," said Immanuel, looking up at Hegel, "yours is not very friendly at all."

"Oh, pay him no mind," replied Hegel. "He just needs something to lift his spirits."

"Well then," said Immanuel, "I have just the thing. What your friend needs is an adventure."

"Adventure?" Hobbes groaned. "You can count me out of that. The world is a frightening enough place as it is. Why would I make it even worse by going on an adventure? They are terrible things."

"They're nothing of the sort," said Immanuel. "Adventures are wonderful, and there's a good chance you might even learn something new."

"Well, I for one have no plans at all today," said Hegel. "I can think of no better way to spend it than going on an adventure with an old friend and a new one."

"There's just one catch," said Immanuel.

"Oh, there's always a catch, isn't there?" asked Hobbes.

"We ants, you see, are known to be hardworking fellows, and I must first move this great pile of seeds back to my home."

"What ... that?" Hobbes asked, looking down at the pile of seeds no taller than his toe. "Why, that's nothing at all."

"For you perhaps, my giant furry friends. But as you've noticed, I am a lot smaller than you, and it will take me all day to move that pile."

"Then let us make a deal," said Hegel. "We will move your seeds for you, and then you will be free to lead us on your adventure."

"You are a very kind hedgehog, and I am happy to accept your offer," said Immanuel. "That is just the sort of deal I had in mind."

Moving Immanuel's seeds took just a few seconds. Hegel simply scooped them up in his furry hand, took five steps across the grass, and dropped them down next to the anthill. He even moved the ones Immanuel had already loaded in his cart.

"Now," said Hegel, "what is this great adventure you have in mind?"

"Oh, it will be something special indeed," Immanuel replied. "And the very best part is that not only will you get to see something new and wonderful, you'll also get to meet another new friend."

"Oh, that's just great," said Hobbes. "I really should have stayed in bed today. First it's a new ant friend, then an adventure, and now another friend? Good grief, when will it ever end?"

"If you're lucky," replied Hegel, "it will never ever end. You will make new friends and have exciting adventures for your entire life."

"What a horrid thought," Hobbes said.

"Is he going to be like this all day?" Immanuel asked, smiling at Hegel.

"I'm afraid it's quite possible," said Hegel. "But tell us about this new friend. Is he a part of the adventure?"

"He most certainly is, and a more unusual friend you will never meet. His name is Plato."

"Plato?" asked Hobbes. "What a strange name. Is he an ant like you?"

"Oh no," Immanuel said. "He is … a bit odd and takes a little getting used to. For starters, he is quite fond of swimming."

"Ah," said Hegel, "so, your friend is a fish."

"I don't much care for fish," said Hobbes. "They're very slimy."

"Oh no, he is most definitely not a fish, and he would have a good laugh to hear you say so. No, no, he is covered in fur just the same as both of you."

At this, both Hobbes and Hegel made curious faces.

"So he's a furry fish?" Hobbes asked. "Now that would be something new."

"No, I've told you, Plato is not a fish. He has a long beak."

"Well then, he is a bird," declared Hobbes.

"A bird that swims," added Hegel.

"A bird that swims and is covered with fur," said Hobbes. Both friends looked at each other in confusion.

"Actually," said Immanuel, "it's not so much a beak as a wide bill."

"Ah, now we're getting somewhere," said Hegel. "Your friend Plato is a duck, but a furry duck."

"I've never met a duck," said Hobbes. "But I've seen them, and they're not furry at all. Hegel, I believe your new friend the ant is trying his best to confuse us."

During all this talk, Hegel and Hobbes had been walking through the garden, with Immanuel perched atop Hegel's head so he wouldn't fall behind. They passed through the great hedge that marked the back of the garden and began making their way across the meadow that lay beyond. Hobbes looked about with a frightened expression.

"We've never been beyond the garden," he said. "What if there are monsters out here?"

"Don't be silly," said Hegel. "Monsters are made up."

"I don't know," Hobbes squealed, his eyes darting about. "Immanuel's friend sounds like a monster — a great furry duck-faced swimming monster. And I cannot believe you let me be talked into coming all this way."

After a good bit more walking and talking, the three friends came to the edge of a small pond in the middle of the meadow.

"Stop here," said Immanuel. "He should be here soon."

And sure enough, after a few more seconds of standing and looking about, there came a small splashing noise from the far side of the pond.

"Here he comes now," shouted Immanuel.

A moment later, there was a large creature with wet fur and a bill just like a duck. He climbed out of the water and waddled up to the three friends.

"Well," he said to Immanuel, "you said you'd come, and here you are."

"My friends," Immanuel said, "may I present Plato the Platypus."

Plato smiled broadly and made a great bow.

"It is my great pleasure to meet you both," he said. "What has Immanuel here told you about me?"

"He said you were a strange fur-covered beast with a bill like a duck, who is not a fish, but who likes to swim," Hobbes said.

"Hold on," said Immanuel. "I never said he was strange."

"Oh, it's all right," Plato said. "I've been called worse. And I am a bit of an odd duck, at least in this neighborhood."

"There, you see," cried Hobbes. "He admits he's a duck!"

"No, Hobbes. That's just a figure of speech," Hegel replied.

"Well anyway," said Hobbes, "now that we're all here and so very far from home, what is this adventure we're supposed to be having?"

"Ah," said Plato, shaking more water off his fur, "a creature after my own heart—right to the point. I have told Immanuel here that if you are brave enough, I can show you a place no creature in this meadow or your garden has ever seen."

"It already sounds terrifying," moaned Hobbes.

Plato turned and pointed to a small island in the center of the pond. "Over there is a wonderful place, where an even more wonderful adventure awaits."

"What?" cried Hobbes. "On the island? How on earth do you mean for us to get there? It may be easy for you, but none of us are furry duck-billed fish who are good swimmers."

"Which is why we must all work together on this adventure," said Plato. "I will take care of getting us to the island. Once we are there, the rest will be up to all of us together. You'll see what I mean once we get there."

"But what is this wondrous thing you keep talking about?" asked Hegel.

"That, my new friends, will be a surprise until we arrive," said Plato.

"But you have not yet told us how we will make it across the pond," said Hegel.

"Easy enough," Plato said. "I shall carry you myself."

"I just knew he was going to say something like that," whined Hobbes. "He expects us all to ride there on his slippery furry back. We must trust that he won't dump us into the water on the way."

"I'm a very good swimmer," Plato replied. "And I shall be very still getting across. You won't even know you've left the land."

"But what if I do not want to go?" asked Hobbes. "What if

I would rather stay here and leave you three to have this adventure on your own?"

"Now, now," said Immanuel, "just think of all the fun you'll miss. If the adventure is a good thing for some of us, then surely it will be an even better thing if we all go."

"And besides," said Hegel, smiling, "we have come a very long way to have this adventure. Wouldn't it be a pity to miss out now?"

"Also," added Plato, "the hardest part of having an adventure is making up your mind to do it. Before you know it, it will be over and you'll be telling all your other friends about it."

Hobbes thought about all of this. He could see that his friends were trying very hard to convince him. Finally he frowned uncertainly and then nodded in agreement.

"Your adventure will probably be the death of me," he moaned, "but at least I'll have company."

"That's the spirit!" Plato said, stepping toward the water's edge.

And so the three friends climbed onto the platypus' back. Hobbes sat behind, holding on for his life. Hegel sat in front so that he wouldn't poke his friend with his sharp fur, and Immanuel sat perched atop Plato's head.

Just as he had promised, Plato glided across the pond. He kept his back steady as he could, to ensure that his friends stayed dry. In only a few minutes they were safe and sound on the beach at the edge of the island.

"And now look," said Plato. "You've made it to a place never before visited by hamster or hedgehog."

"And never again," huffed Hobbes. "These adventures are not at all to my liking."

"Come, come," Plato said, waddling his way up the beach. "I want to show you why we have come all this way."

The friends walked a short distance to where a lone tree stood. Its branches were covered with what looked from a distance like small red dots. As they drew nearer, the truth became clear.

"Goodness, look," said Hegel happily. "Why, it's filled with apples!"

And so it was. The tree was so filled with ripe red apples that the lower branches hung very close to the ground. Plato waddled to the lowest branch of all and raised himself up as high as he could. But his tiny arm was still a few inches away from the nearest reddest apple.

"And so now you see why we have all come," he said, lowering himself back to the ground. "I am an excellent swimmer, but I'm afraid I am no climber."

"Well, I'm of no help," said Hobbes. "I've never climbed a thing in my life."

"Nor have I," agreed Hegel. "We hedgehogs are ground creatures."

"I am a very good climber," said Immanuel. But then he sighed sadly. "But it is a terribly long way, and I am tiny. I'd be all day getting up there and to the apples. And even then, what could I do except take a bite for myself?"

"That," said Plato, "is why we are going to have to work to-gether if we are to enjoy this wonderful fruit."

"How do you imagine we can do it?" asked Hegel. "It's very high."

"I have given this a good deal of thought," said Plato, facing his friends. "And here is my plan. I cannot reach the branch by myself because, even though I am the largest, I am still too short."

"Which means that none of the rest of us can do any better," said Immanuel.

"That is true," smiled Plato, "but if we combine our heights, we can reach the apples easily."

"Oh, I don't like the sound of that one little bit," moaned Hobbes. "Can't you see what he means to do?"

"I do," replied Hegel. "I think I do indeed. We shall stand one atop the other and then pull down all the apples we like."

"And because a hamster is smaller than a hedgehog, and a hedgehog is smaller than a platypus, you will no doubt expect me to stand at the top of the whole thing."

"Well, not quite," said Plato. "It is true you are smaller

than Hegel or myself. But Immanuel here is the very smallest of all. He can stand on top of Hobbes. Then he can climb up onto the branch, chew through the stems with his strong jaws, and drop the apples to the ground."

Hobbes looked uncertainly at Hegel. "Is this the sort of thing that normally happens on adventures?" he asked.

"Well," said Hegel, "I've not been on many myself, but yes, I think so."

"I don't like it one little bit," replied Hobbes, "especially the part about being at the very top of the pile."

"Don't forget," said Immanuel, "I'm the one who has to go climbing up into the tree."

"How is it that our new platypus friend here gets to suggest the plan, but then he gets to stand safely at the bottom of the pile?" asked Hobbes.

"No matter," replied Plato. "I am happy to climb to the top of the pile, and we can stand on Hobbes' back."

Hobbes frowned at this idea and grudgingly agreed to Plato's plan.

"All right then," Plato said, "let us fetch some apples, for I am very hungry from all the swimming and talking."

He bent down and let Hegel climb onto his shoulders. And the hedgehog, of course, took great care not to poke his new friend with his sharp spines. Then Hobbes climbed atop Hegel's shoulders, and Immanuel climbed onto Hobbes' head. Finally Plato carefully stood up, with all of his friends on his shoulders, and moved toward the biggest reddest apple. As he drew closer, the entire pile began to sway unsteadily, first in one direction, then another.

"Hold steady!" Hobbes shouted from high atop the group. "You'll kill us all."

"So sorry," Plato said, puffing with the weight of his friends. "I was only trying to bring us closer."

Plato moved more carefully until he was standing directly beneath a large low-hanging apple. Immanuel crept up Hobbes' outstretched hand and leapt easily onto the branch. As he jumped, the pile with Plato, Hegel, and Hobbes became unsteady and spun to one side. Hegel tumbled off from Plato's head onto the grass below. Plato and Hegel stood up, brushed themselves off, and looked about.

"Where did Hobbes go?" Hegel asked with alarm.

"I'm up here, for heaven's sake," came a voice from far above their heads.

The two looked up to see Hobbes hanging from the tree branch above. "And I don't expect I can hang on much longer. So if it's not too much trouble, could you climb back up and bring me down?"

While Hegel was climbing once more onto Plato's head, Immanuel was busily chewing through apple stems. Every few seconds a fresh red apple would fall to the ground. One very nearly upset Plato and Hegel as they worked to rescue the stranded Hobbes. In only a moment, Hobbes was safely back atop Hegel's head, and Immanuel had scurried back down and onto the ground. Seconds later, all four were safely on the grass, happily munching away at the apples they had harvested.

"I thought for sure I was doomed," Hobbes said, his mouth filled with juicy apple.

"It is quite possible," said Plato, "that you are the very first hamster ever to climb a tree."

Hobbes smiled at the thought. "And the first, as well, to swim across a raging pond."

The four friends turned and looked out across the pond, its water barely moving in the bright morning sun. All at once they began laughing so hard that they rolled about in the grass, clutching at their apple-filled bellies.

"It almost makes me wonder what our next adventure will be like," Hobbes said, lying back and letting the bright morning sun warm his soft fur.

Sarah Drake is an illustrator and artist living in San Antonio, Texas. An avid animal lover, her childhood pets became art subjects and models for her sketches and paintings. Sarah has written and illustrated several books, and has been a guest artist in area schools to inspire other young artists and entrepreneurs. Many of her paintings, creations, and illustrations can be seen and purchased on her website *Sarah's Curious Creations*.

Brian Kenneth Swain is the author of eight books, including the novels *World Hunger, Alone in the Light,* and *Sistina*; the poetry collections *Secret Places, My America,* and *Chicken Feet*; the short story collection *The Book of Names*; and the essay collection *The Curious Habits of Man*. His writing has been featured on NPR and Pacifica Radio. He lives in San Antonio with his black chow chows Maya and Loki.

Lightning Source UK Ltd.
Milton Keynes UK
UKHW052349200520
363426UK00006B/124

9 781532 099700